Mixed Us

A Tale of Two Mixed Girls

Cheatie Holeman

ISBN: Softcover   978-1-5245-2989-5
        EBook   978-1-5245-2988-8

Print information available on the last page

Rev. date: 07/28/2016

To order additional copies of this book, contact:
Xlibris
1-888-795-4274
www.Xlibris.com
Orders@Xlibris.com

We have two grandmoms' one black and one white.
They are as different as day and night.

We live with our Caucasian mother and brothers.
We all get along like peanut butter and jelly.

One weekend we visit our white grandma and
eat good food that she cooks just right.

The next weekend we spend with our black grandma. She knows when she feeds us we will be coming back.

Our Grandmas are different as wrong and right. We have never heard them argue, fuss or fight.

One grandma is fast the other is slow. When we have a question we know where to go.
They both read the paper and sing us a song and when they make a mistake they both say "ding dong."

Our grandmas are smart and sometimes play dumb, one sucks her finger the other sucks her thumb.

Our grandmas are different like a sock and a shoe, but when
we do something wrong they both know what to do.

They don't spank us, they make us feel bad.
If one of us gets punished and we all feel sad.

When our punishment is over, we are back having fun. With either grandma it's over and done.

Our mom and dad's families are different as the
sky and the sea. But we love them all like the
birds in the trees because they all look like

MIXED US!

They shower us with love, no
matter the day or time. When
they leave us to go away
That's when we start to whine.

Our Grandmas are good, we both have the best.
Neither is better because they make us clean up our mess.

They teach us to cook, clean and have fun
and when it is bedtime
we try and run.

12

Black Grandma - makes us brush our teeth and
take a bath.

She knows when we are sleepy because
we both start to laugh.

We laugh about nothing and at anything at all,
because we know it's time to
end a good day, we both had a ball.

13

White Grandma - Lets us eat a snack and
make a mess
because tomorrow is a new day
and we are getting our rest.

We said our Grandmas are different like the night and the day
but we love them dearly because they let us have our way.

Our Grandmas are different like democratic and republicans.
They disagree sometimes like sister and brother.

One voted for Hillary the other for Trump we don't know the difference so we just stomp.

One talks about politics the other about life. It doesn't mean a thing to us because we are too young to strife.

We learn from the two of them
in a way we think it's grand.
We are learning to be black and to be white
but we know we are learning everything that is right.

WE are **MIXED US**

Black and white we know because we are
granddaughters of **MIXED US**, for sho'.

We know we're half black, we are also half white,
we may have some chinese
but we have a great life.

Acknowledgements

Thank you to all who have helped me with this children's book. To my precious granddaughters who are teaching me to have patience at my age, to my sister, Thelma and coworkers who read the book and said it was good, to my friend and editor who tell me what to say and do and finally to all my family and friends who kept me motivated.
I love you all.
More to come I hope.

MomMom White, aka Cheatie, aka Fairy

Printed in the United States
by Baker & Taylor Publisher Services